Acting Edition

A Doll's House

by Henrik Ibsen

A New Version
by Amy Herzog

No one shall make any changes in this title(s) for the purpose of production. No part of this book may be reproduced, stored in a retrieval system, scanned, uploaded, or transmitted in any form, by any means, now known or yet to be invented, including mechanical, electronic, digital, photocopying, recording, videotaping, or otherwise, without the prior written permission of the publisher. No one shall share this title(s), or any part of this title(s), through any social media or file hosting websites.

For all inquiries regarding motion picture, television, online/digital and other media rights, please contact Concord Theatricals Corp.

MUSIC AND THIRD-PARTY MATERIALS USE NOTE

Licensees are solely responsible for obtaining formal written permission from copyright owners to use copyrighted music and/or other copyrighted third-party materials (e.g. recordings, artworks, logos) in the performance of this play and are strongly cautioned to do so. If no such permission is obtained by the licensee, then the licensee must use only original music and materials that the licensee owns and controls. Licensees are solely responsible and liable for clearances of all third-party copyrighted materials, including without limitation music, and shall indemnify the copyright owners of the play(s) and their licensing agent, Concord Theatricals Corp., against any costs, expenses, losses and liabilities arising from the use of such copyrighted third-party materials by licensees. For music, please contact the appropriate music licensing authority in your territory for the rights to any incidental music.

IMPORTANT BILLING AND CREDIT REQUIREMENTS

If you have obtained performance rights to this title, please refer to your licensing agreement for important billing and credit requirements.

The Original Broadway Production of *A DOLL'S HOUSE* was produced by Ambassador Theatre Group Productions, Gavin Kalin Productions, Wessex Grove, Julie Boardman, Kate Cannova, Bob Boyett, Hunter Arnold, Creative Partners Productions, Eilene Davidson Productions, GGRS, Kater Gordon, Louise L. Gund, Los Angeles Media Fund, Stephanie P. McClelland, Tilted, Jessica Chastain, Caitlin Clements/Francesca Moody Productions, Caiola Productions/Amanda Lee, Ted & Richard Liebowitz/Joeye-Waldorf Squeri, Richard & Cecilia Attias/Thomas S. Barnes, and OHenry Theatre Nerd Productions/Runyonland MMP, and premeiered at the Hudson Theatre, New York, on March 9, 2023. The performance was directed by Jamie Lloyd, with scenic design by Soutra Gilmour, costume design by Enver Chakartash and Soutra Gilmour, lighting design by Jon Clark, and sound design by Ben Ringham and Max Ringham. The Production Stage Manager was Frank Lombardi. The cast was as follows:

NORA HELMER . . . . Jessica Chastain

TORVALD HELMER . . . . Arian Moayed

DOCTOR RANK . . . . Michael Patrick Thornton

KRISTINE LINDE . . . . Jesmille Darbouze

NILS KROGSTAD . . . . Okieriete Onaodowan

ANNE-MARIE . . . . Tasha Lawrence

CHARACTERS

NORA HELMER – a wife and mother

TORVALD HELMER – her husband, a lawyer

DOCTOR RANK – a friend of the Helmers

KRISTINE LINDE – a school friend of Nora's

NILS KROGSTAD – a lawyer

IVAR – seven, Nora and Torvald's son

EMMY – five, Nora and Torvald's daughter

ANNE-MARIE – a nanny

SETTING

Norway.
The Helmers' living room.

TIME

1879.
Three consecutive days at Christmastime.

TRANSLATOR'S NOTE

Ibsen's 1879 masterwork requires very little intervention to be fully legible in 2023. In this new version, I tried to be as faithful as possible to the playwright's intentions, clearing away dramaturgical elements and portions of dialogue that, for a modern audience's sensibilities, can distract from the gathering dramatic momentum. Notably, I cut the character Helene, the maid, whose function in the original is mainly to introduce visitors as they arrive at the Helmer home. I marked these entrances with the simple stage direction "Shift" – a brief time lapse, to be indicated through lighting or otherwise. In addition to doing away with unnecessary exposition, these faster transitions contribute to the sense of Nora's growing anxiety and disorientation as the plot unfolds.

In Jamie Lloyd's Broadway production, there were no props, almost no scenery, no costume changes, and the children were pre-recorded voices. When props were referred to in the dialogue, the actors did not mime or indicate the props in any way; the audience was left to imagine the objects and the actions. I felt this worked beautifully, focusing the audience's attention on the psychology of the characters rather than the stage business. However, it is entirely possible to do a traditional production of the play using this translation, or to find other points on the spectrum between modern dress on an empty stage and a fully realized, period mise-en-scène. I would love to see a range of interpretations in future productions.

A Doll's House is traditionally performed with two intermissions; our production ran just under two hours with no intermission. A single intermission between acts two and three is also possible.

Two other specifics –

In Ibsen's original, Torvald plays the piano for the famous scene where Nora practices the tarantella. In our production, there was no music at all for this scene and Torvald and Dr. Rank just clapped a beat for Nora. I am including supplemental pages that offer the option of Torvald playing piano or playing recorded music for this scene, at the director's discretion.

Ibsen gave Nora and Torvald three children. In this version, I've changed it to just two children to make it more feasible to produce with child actors.

ACT ONE

(The Helmers' living room. Christmas Eve Day.)

*(**NORA** hums, chuckling happily. She's just returned from a successful shopping trip. She whistles a bird call.)*

TORVALD. *(Offstage.)* Do I hear something chirping out there?

NORA. Tweet tweet!

TORVALD. *(Offstage.)* Is that a little bird?

NORA. Yes it is!

(She makes some more bird noises. This is a cute, dorky game they play – the kind of cringey couple behavior that shouldn't really be witnessed by others.)

TORVALD. *(Offstage.)* When did you get home, Birdie?

NORA. A minute ago. Torvald, come out here so I can tell you what I bought!

TORVALD. *(Offstage.)* I'm working!

(But a moment later he appears.)

Did you say "bought"?

NORA. This year we can afford it! It's the first Christmas we don't have such a tight budget –

TORVALD. But we can't be extravagant.

NORA. Oh Torvald we can be a tiny bit extravagant. Can't we? Now that you'll be making tons of money.

TORVALD. After the New Year, but it'll be a few months till my first paycheck.

NORA. So? We can borrow till then.

TORVALD. Nora. What if I borrowed a thousand today and you blew it all and then on New Year's Eve I got hit by lightning –

NORA. Bite your tongue!

TORVALD. Well what if something terrible happened?

NORA. Then I wouldn't care if I owed money or not.

TORVALD. Okay, but what about the people I borrowed from?

NORA. Who cares about them! They're strangers.

TORVALD. You're adorable, but come on, baby, you know how I feel about debt – there's something shameful about it. We've made it this long without begging or borrowing, right? We can stick it out a couple more months.

NORA. Fine.

(She moves away from him. He watches her sulk.)

TORVALD. Are you sulking?

NORA. *(Sulkily.)* No...

TORVALD. You're not?

(She shrugs, not looking at him.)

It's too bad you're mad at me, because...let's see what I have here...

NORA. Cash!

TORVALD. You think I don't know how expensive Christmas is in a house with two kids?

NORA. Thank you, Torvald! I'll make it last.

TORVALD. Yeah, you'll have to.

NORA. I know. But let me tell you, I bought the cutest new sweater for Ivar, and a sword – everything was on sale – a doll and cradle for Emmy, they're cheap but who cares, she'll just destroy them anyway. I got a scarf for Anne-Marie, she really deserves something nicer –

TORVALD. Anything for me?

NORA. Oh no. I knew I forgot something.

TORVALD. What did you get me?

NORA. Not telling! You have to wait till tonight.

TORVALD. Okay, okay. What about you?

NORA. Me?

TORVALD. You, with the holes in your pockets, what did you get yourself?

NORA. Oh, I don't want anything.

TORVALD. Nothing? Come on, let me spoil you a little. Tell me.

NORA. Oh gosh I don't know. Maybe...

TORVALD. Spit it out.

NORA. *(Quickly.)* More cash. Just whatever you can spare, and one of these days I'll get myself something with it.

TORVALD. Nora –

NORA. I'll wrap it in pretty gold paper and hang it on the tree for myself, it'll be fun! And then I'll have time to think about what I need. Come on, that's very reasonable!

TORVALD. Except that somehow it'll just disappear and then you'll come right back for / more.

NORA. That's not fair! I really try to save everything I can.

TORVALD. That's true – you try. You just can't.

NORA. You know, you actually have no idea, the expenses a little bird like me has.

TORVALD. You're just like your father. Money slips through your fingers – you don't even know what you did with it. Well – for richer or for poorer, right?

NORA. I wish I were more like Papa.

TORVALD. And I wouldn't change a single thing about you, Birdie. I mean that.

(He watches her for a moment.)

What's going on with you today?

NORA. What do you mean?

TORVALD. You look kind of...

NORA. What?

TORVALD. Kind of guilty.

NORA. I do?

TORVALD. Look at me.

(She does.)

While you were out today, did you by some chance... succumb to a sugar craving?

NORA. Of course not.

TORVALD. You didn't accidentally wander into a bakery? Nibble a pastry or two?

NORA. No –

TORVALD. Or buy some cookies and smuggle them / into the –?

NORA. Torvald, I swear –

TORVALD. I'm just teasing you.

NORA. I would never go behind your back like that.

TORVALD. I know, you promised. You can keep your little Christmas secrets. I'll find out everything later when we light up the tree.

NORA. Did you remember to invite Peter to dinner?

TORVALD. I don't need to, he'll be there. But I'll mention it when he drops by this morning. I ordered some good wine. God, I'm looking forward to tonight, Nora.

NORA. Me too. And the kids are going to love it.

TORVALD. It's amazing to finally have a job with some security, right? To make real money.

NORA. We've waited so long for this.

TORVALD. Remember last Christmas? When you locked yourself up every night for three weeks making ornaments to surprise us? The most boring three weeks of my life.

NORA. Not for me.

TORVALD. And all your hard work was much appreciated... by the cat.

NORA. Stop! It wasn't my fault Smokey got in at the last minute and tore everything up.

TORVALD. No, it's the thought that counts. Thank God those tough times are over.

NORA. Is it really true? Am I dreaming?

TORVALD. It's real. You'll never have to work like that again. We'll have what we want –

NORA. I have this idea for a renovation, Torvald, can I tell you? Maybe we could –

(*The doorbell rings.*)

Shoot.

TORVALD. I'm not home.

(*Shift.* **TORVALD** *exits.* **KRISTINE** *comes before* **NORA**.)

KRISTINE. Hello, Nora.

NORA. Hello…

KRISTINE. You don't recognize me?

NORA. I'm sorry, I'm not sure I – wait a second –

Kristine! Is it really you?

KRISTINE. It's me.

NORA. I can't I believe I didn't recognize you! But – you look different.

KRISTINE. I'm sure I do. It's been nine, ten years –

NORA. It hasn't been that long, has it? God, it has. The last eight have been so happy for us it's kind of a blur and I didn't – but here you are! You traveled all the way here in winter, that was brave.

KRISTINE. I just arrived this morning.

NORA. To celebrate Christmas in the city! Oh, we're going to have fun. Come sit, it's cozy over here. Now you look like yourself! It was just at first – you're thinner than you used to be, that's all.

KRISTINE. Also older. Much older.

NORA. Maybe a tiny bit, not much – no, not at all!

(*She stops suddenly, mortified.*)

How could I be so insensitive, chattering on like a – Kristine, can you forgive me?

KRISTINE. For what?

NORA. You lost your husband.

KRISTINE. Yes. Three years ago.

NORA. I meant to write to you so many times, but I kept putting it off till I had time and there was never time –

KRISTINE. I completely understand –

NORA. No it was horrible of me. You poor thing, you've been through so much. And he didn't leave you any money?

KRISTINE. No.

NORA. And no children?

KRISTINE. None.

NORA. So nothing, then.

KRISTINE. No, not even grief.

NORA. That can't be true.

KRISTINE. Oh, it does happen sometimes, Nora.

NORA. So you're completely alone. I have two sweet little ones, you'll meet them later, they're out with the nanny. So tell me everything –

KRISTINE. No, you talk.

NORA. No you! I'm not going to be selfish today. Today I'm only going to think about you. But first I have to tell you one thing! Maybe you've already heard?

KRISTINE. No, what?

NORA. It's unbelievable, my husband was just named manager of the Savings Bank.

KRISTINE. Really! You must be thrilled.

NORA. We are. Being a lawyer is such an unstable way of making a living these days, especially if you'll only take clients who are completely honest and above board, which is how Torvald is and I totally agree with him. I still can't believe it. He starts at the bank in the New Year and he'll get a big salary plus commissions and everything. It's life-changing, we'll be able to do whatever we want. Kristine, I can't tell you how much lighter I feel. Doesn't that sound dreamy, to have lots of money and never have to worry again??

KRISTINE. It does sound nice, to be able to afford the necessities.

NORA. No, not just the necessities, Kristine, tons and tons of money!

KRISTINE. You haven't changed at all! In school you were already famous for spending money.

NORA. Torvald says I'm still like that. But I've changed a lot, actually. I've had to save every penny so we could make ends meet. And we both had to work.

KRISTINE. You worked too?

NORA. Surprised? Yes. Little things, needlework, crocheting...other things. Torvald left his government job when we got married, that wasn't going anywhere and we needed more money. But that first year he took on all these extra jobs, worked himself to the bone, and it almost killed him, he got so sick. The doctors said he absolutely had to travel south.

KRISTINE. Italy, right?

NORA. Yes, we went for a year. It wasn't easy to figure out, believe me. Ivar had just been born. But obviously we had no choice. It was wonderful, actually. And it saved Torvald's life. But it cost so much money, Kristine.

KRISTINE. I can imagine.

NORA. Four thousand eight hundred. A *lot* of money.

KRISTINE. Thank goodness you had it.

NORA. We didn't. We got it from Papa.

KRISTINE. That must have been right around the time your father passed –

NORA. Exactly, in fact I couldn't be with Papa when he was dying, I was nine months pregnant with Ivar and nursing Torvald at the same time. I never saw my sweet, kind Papa again! That's the hardest thing I've been through since getting married.

KRISTINE. I'm sorry, I remember how close you were. But...then you left for Italy?

NORA. Right – then we had the money, and the doctors insisted. And thank God, Torvald was completely cured.

KRISTINE. But...the *doctor*...

NORA. Sorry?

KRISTINE. I arrived at the same time as a man – I thought he said "Doctor" –

NORA. Oh that must have been Dr. Rank – but he's not making a house call, Peter's our best friend and he comes every day. No, Torvald hasn't had a sniffle since then. And the children and I are healthy too, thank God. Kristine, it's so good to be alive and feel hopeful! Oh no I'm doing it again, I'm talking about myself. Don't be mad at me. Is it really true you weren't in love with your husband? Why did you marry him?

KRISTINE. My mother was sick and house-bound, I had to take care of her and my younger brothers. I couldn't think of a good reason to refuse his offer.

NORA. So he was rich?

KRISTINE. I think he was pretty well off then, but his business was shaky and by the time he died he was bankrupt.

NORA. What did you do?

KRISTINE. I managed a shop and then a small school and some other things. The last three years has been like one long workday. But now it's over. My mother passed. The boys don't need me anymore, they're grown up and have their own jobs.

NORA. You must feel so relieved.

KRISTINE. No; just utterly empty. No one to live for. That's why I left, there was no reason to stay out in the middle of nowhere. It should be easier to find a job in the city, preferably office work –

NORA. But that sounds exhausting and you already look so tired. What you need is a few months at a spa somewhere.

KRISTINE. I don't have a Papa who can finance my vacations.

NORA. Kristine…I'm sorry –

KRISTINE. No, I'm sorry. The worst part about what I've been through is that it's made me bitter. I've spent too much time alone, I've become…self-pitying…

NORA. No, you're being too –

KRISTINE. When you told me your good news – I'm ashamed to admit this, but I was happier for myself than for you.

NORA. What do you mean? Oh. You think Torvald might do something for you.

KRISTINE. I thought maybe…

NORA. He will! I'd love to help you, I truly would. Watch, I'll bring it up in a way that makes him feel…you'll see!

KRISTINE. It's kind of you to take such an interest in me, Nora. Especially since life has been so easy on you.

NORA. On me? "So easy..."

KRISTINE. I know, you had to do some needlework, but – Nora, you're basically still a child.

NORA. You shouldn't be so condescending.

KRISTINE. Excuse me?

NORA. You all think I'm helpless when it comes to serious –

KRISTINE. I didn't say that –

NORA. That I've never really *done* anything, I haven't struggled –

KRISTINE. But you just told me all about your struggles.

NORA. That? That was nothing.

(Quietly.) I didn't tell you the big thing.

KRISTINE. What big thing? What are you talking about?

NORA. You shouldn't look down on me, Kristine. You're proud that you worked hard to take care of your mother.

KRISTINE. I don't look down on anyone. But you're right, I'm proud that I was able to make my mother's last years comfortable.

NORA. And you're proud of the sacrifices you made for your brothers.

KRISTINE. I think I have a right to be.

NORA. I agree. But Kristine, I've earned the right to feel proud too.

KRISTINE. I'm sure you have. But what do you mean?

NORA. We have to be quiet. Imagine if Torvald heard! He can never, ever – promise you won't tell anyone.

KRISTINE. Tell what?

NORA. *(Pause.)* I saved Torvald's life.

KRISTINE. What do you mean, "saved"?

NORA. If I hadn't taken him to Italy he would have –

KRISTINE. Right, but your father gave you the money –

NORA. Mm-hm, that's what Torvald and everyone else thinks, but...

KRISTINE. But?

NORA. Papa didn't give us a penny. I found the money.

KRISTINE. All that money?

NORA. Four thousand eight hundred.

KRISTINE. ...did you win the lottery?

NORA. The lottery! That doesn't take any skill!

KRISTINE. Then where did you get it?

(**NORA** *smiles, enjoying this.*)

Because you couldn't borrow it!

NORA. Why not?

KRISTINE. A woman needs her husband's consent.

NORA. Unless that woman happened to have a little business sense, if she happened to be resourceful and smart –

KRISTINE. I don't understand –

NORA. That's fine. I never said I borrowed the money. I could have gotten it a million other ways.

(*She preens.*)

From some admirer, for example. With these looks...

KRISTINE. You're out of your mind.

NORA. And you're dying to know my secret, aren't you?

KRISTINE. Please tell me you didn't do something rash.

NORA. Is it rash to save your husband's life?

KRISTINE. It might be, if you went behind his back and –

NORA. But I wasn't allowed to tell him anything! He couldn't even know how sick he was. The doctors came to *me* saying he would die, that the only thing that could save him was this trip. You think I didn't try a hundred other ways to convince him? I pleaded with him to take me on a romantic trip to Italy, like some of my school friends had done with their husbands. I told him *I* needed to recover after giving birth, I cried and begged, and I brought up the idea of a loan...but that made him furious, he said it was his duty as my husband not to give in to my whims. Well, I thought. You're not allowed to die, so I'll just have to figure something out. And I did.

KRISTINE. Your father never let it slip that the money didn't come from him?

NORA. Papa was dying right at the same time. He would have kept my secret, but I never got the chance to tell him.

KRISTINE. And you didn't ever tell Torvald?

NORA. You don't know how strict he is! His pride – no, he'd be humiliated, to think he owed me anything. Our marriage would never be the same.

KRISTINE. Will you tell him someday?

NORA. *(Pensive, half-smiling.)* Maybe. When we're older and I'm not as attractive. Then it might be a good idea to have something up my sleeve –

(She suddenly breaks off.)

What am I talking about! That's never going to happen. So! What do you think, Kristine? Are you impressed with me? By the way, it's been incredibly stressful. It turns out in business, there's something called "quarterly interest," and something else called "monthly installments" and I'm always in a panic to find the money. I couldn't squeeze anything out of the household budget because Torvald has to live a certain way, and I couldn't bear to skimp on the children's clothes, it's not *their* fault –

KRISTINE. So it came out of your own share.

NORA. It had to. Whenever Torvald gave me money for my clothes, I only spent half, bought the cheapest materials. Thank God everything looks good on me so he didn't notice. But it's been hard! I want to wear nice things, don't you?

KRISTINE. Well, sure…

NORA. And I've had some jobs here and there, like I said. Last Christmas I got a big copying job, I stayed up late writing every night for weeks. It was exhausting, but it was also fun, to work hard and make money! I felt kind of like a man.

KRISTINE. How much have you been able to pay back?

NORA. I'm not exactly sure, it's impossible to keep track. All I know is that I've paid every cent I could. Sometimes I almost lost hope. Then I'd fantasize that this rich older man fell in love with me –

KRISTINE. What! Who?

NORA. And that he suddenly died and when they opened his will it said in huge letters "I LEAVE EVERYTHING TO THE FABULOUS NORA HELMER, WHO SHOULD BE PAID IMMEDIATELY IN CASH."

KRISTINE. So who is he?

NORA. Kristine – he was just a daydream I had when I couldn't make the payments! Anyway, isn't it incredible, that the worry is over and I'm totally free? I can play with the children all day and make the house perfect for Torvald. Then spring will come, and maybe we can even travel. Maybe I'll get to see the ocean again!

(The doorbell rings.)

KRISTINE. I should go –

NORA. No stay! It's probably someone for Torvald – I don't know who it could be –

*(Shift. **KROGSTAD** is there.)*

KROGSTAD. It's me.

*(**KRISTINE** startles slightly, then turns away. **NORA** visibly tenses.)*

I'd like to speak to your husband.

(A pause.)

NORA. What about?

KROGSTAD. Bank business. I have a job at the Savings Bank and I just heard your husband is our new manager.

NORA. Oh. I didn't realize…

*(**NORA** hesitates.)*

KROGSTAD. I'm only here to discuss tedious business matters, Mrs. Helmer. That's all.

NORA. His office is through there.

*(**KROGSTAD** exits.)*

KRISTINE. Who was that?

NORA. Uh, Mr. Krogstad, he's a lawyer.

KRISTINE. That's what I thought.

NORA. You know him?

KRISTINE. I used to. He was a clerk for a judge in my town, years ago. He's changed.

NORA. He was in a terrible marriage, apparently.

KRISTINE. Widowed?

NORA. With a bunch of children.

KRISTINE. He works a lot of...different kinds of jobs? Is that right?

NORA. Maybe, I wouldn't know. Let's not talk about business, it's too boring.

(**RANK** *enters.*)

RANK. *(To Torvald, offstage.)* No, I'll get out of your way! I'll visit with your better half.

(*He sees* **KRISTINE.**)

Oh, I'm in your way, too.

NORA. Never. Dr. Rank – this is Kristine Linde.

RANK. Oh hello! I've been hearing that name for years. I'm sorry I didn't realize – I think I passed you on my way in.

KRISTINE. I'm moving slowly these days.

RANK. A little under the weather?

KRISTINE. Just exhausted, I think.

RANK. *(Gentle teasing.)* So you've come to the big city for some peace and quiet?

KRISTINE. No, I'm looking for a job.

RANK. I'm not sure that's medically recommended for exhaustion.

KRISTINE. Well, one has to live.

RANK. That does seem to be the general consensus.

NORA. Come on Peter, you want to live too.

RANK. Guilty. No matter how miserable I am, I want to extend my suffering as long as possible. My patients are the same way. And the same goes for people with moral diseases. Speaking of...

NORA. Speaking of what?

RANK. That lawyer Krogstad – you don't know him, he's your garden variety degenerate. But he just walked in saying the same thing, that he "has to live," as if it were a matter of great importance.

NORA. What did he want to talk to Torvald about?

RANK. I don't know, something about the Savings Bank. I guess he has a job there.

(To **KRISTINE**, *ironically.)* I'm not sure if it's the same where you come from, but here in the city when we discover someone is morally sick, what we do is we elevate them into a competitive job – as treatment, you understand. The decent, healthy people have to fend for themselves.

KRISTINE. I guess it's the sick who most need to be cared for.

RANK. There you go. And that attitude is exactly what's turned modern society into a hospital.

(Suddenly, **NORA** *laughs.)*

What's so funny? What do you know about modern society?

NORA. So everyone who works at the Savings Bank – now works for Torvald?

RANK. Is that what you find hilarious?

NORA. Maybe. Don't you worry about it.

(A beat.)

It's so fun to think that we – that Torvald has power over so many people. Want a cookie?

*(***RANK** *gasps performatively.)*

RANK. I thought those were contraband.

NORA. Oh Kristine brought me these.

KRISTINE. What?

NORA. It's okay, you didn't know that Torvald banned them. He's afraid they'll rot my teeth. But just this once won't hurt, right, Doctor?

(*To* **KRISTINE**.) And one for you. And one for me…and one more for me…I really couldn't be happier. Almost. Except there's one more thing I'm dying to do.

RANK. Do tell.

NORA. I have such a naughty urge to say something shocking in front of Torvald.

KRISTINE. Shocking?

RANK. You'd better not. But you can try it out on us. Go ahead.

NORA. I'm just bursting to say…

Fuck it all.

RANK. Ha!

KRISTINE. Nora!

(**TORVALD** *is entering.*)

RANK. Do it! Here's your opportunity.

NORA. Did you get rid of him?

TORVALD. Yes, he's gone.

NORA. Torvald, this is Kristine, she just got here.

TORVALD. Kristine – I'm sorry, have we –

NORA. Kristine Linde, my friend Kristine –

TORVALD. (*Covering.*) Uh-huh! You were childhood friends, is that right?

KRISTINE. We've known each other a long time.

NORA. And now Kristine has made this long journey in the dead of winter and she did it just for the opportunity to speak to you.

TORVALD. To me?

KRISTINE. Well –

NORA. Kristine is very talented at office work and in order to perfect her skills she's looking for a mentor, a man who can teach her everything / she –

TORVALD. That's very smart.

NORA. And when she heard you were appointed bank manager – it was in the paper – she got on the first train here, and – Torvald, couldn't you help her, it would mean so much to me –

TORVALD. You know, maybe I could. You're a widow?

KRISTINE. Yes.

TORVALD. And you have office experience?

KRISTINE. Many years.

TORVALD. Well...then I can probably help you.

NORA. See! I told you!

TORVALD. You came at the right time, Mrs. Linde.

KRISTINE. I don't know how to thank you.

TORVALD. You don't need to. But I'm sorry, I have to go out now –

RANK. Wait, I'm coming too.

NORA. *(To* **TORVALD.***)* Don't stay out long.

TORVALD. I'll be back in less than an hour.

NORA. Are you leaving too, Kristine?

KRISTINE. I have to find somewhere to stay.

TORVALD. We can all walk out together, then.

NORA. It's so annoying that we don't have a guest room –
I wish we could –

KRISTINE. Stop! Goodbye, and thank you.

NORA. Come back tonight!

(*To* **RANK.**) You too. You're feeling up to it, right? You'll
be fine, just dress warmly.

(**CHILDREN**'s *voices in the hallway.*)

Here they are! Come in, come in!

(**IVAR** *and* **EMMY** *enter with* **ANNE-MARIE.**)

Hi sweethearts!

(*To* **KRISTINE,** *over the* **CHILDREN**'s *voices.*) That's Ivar
and that's little Emmy – aren't they too much?

RANK. We're letting the cold air in.

TORVALD. Let's get out while we still can.

(**TORVALD, KRISTINE,** *and* **RANK** *leave in a
hurry.*)

NORA. Your cheeks are pink! Are you so so cold?

IVAR. Mama, I pulled Emmy on the sled!

NORA. You're so strong! Give me this baby doll.

EMMY. I threw snowballs!

NORA. You did?

ANNE-MARIE. I'll take them to get changed.

NORA. Not yet, I'll play with them for a bit.

ANNE-MARIE. Are you sure?

NORA. You look half frozen, go make yourself some /
coffee. Go.

(**ANNE-MARIE** *exits.*)

IVAR. A dog chased us. I thought he was going to bite us but / he was just playing.

NORA. No, dogs don't bite my little ones, they wouldn't dare.

IVAR. Can we play hide and seek?

NORA. Sure! Who should hide first?

IVAR. You.

EMMY. Mama hide!

NORA. Fine, go in there and count.

> (*The* **CHILDREN** *go into an adjacent room and can be heard counting to ten.*)

> (*In the meantime,* **NORA** *hides.*)

IVAR. Ready or not –

IVAR & EMMY. HERE WE COME!

> (*The* **CHILDREN** *come in and see no sign of* **NORA**.*)*

> (*Silence. An uncanny moment – where could their mother be?*)

EMMY. Mama?

> (*They look around for her.*)

Mama?

> (**NORA** *sneaks back in behind them.*)

NORA. Here / I am!

> (*The* **CHILDREN** *scream! And then laugh as she tackles them.*)

> (*There's a knock at the front door, but they don't hear it, they're in a tickle pile.*)

NORA. All right, now one of you hide.

(**KROGSTAD** *enters uncertainly.*)

KROGSTAD. Excuse me.

(**NORA** *shrieks.*)

Someone must have left the door open. I did knock –

NORA. My husband's not here.

KROGSTAD. I know. Can we talk?

(*A brief pause.*)

NORA. (*To the* **CHILDREN.**) Go to Anne-Marie.

EMMY. / No!

IVAR. But –

NORA. We'll play after the man leaves, go ahead. Now. *Now.*

(*The* **CHILDREN** *exit.*)

What? It's not the first of the month yet.

KROGSTAD. No, it's Christmas Eve. I'd like to have a nice Christmas. I'm sure you would, too.

NORA. What do you want? I don't have your money tod–

KROGSTAD. I'm here about something else. You have a few minutes?

NORA. Well...apparently.

KROGSTAD. Good. I was having lunch down the street and I saw your husband walk by –

NORA. Mm-hm.

KROGSTAD. With a woman.

NORA. So?

KROGSTAD. Can I ask, was that Kristine Linde?

NORA. Yes.

KROGSTAD. Did she just get to town?

NORA. This morning. Why?

KROGSTAD. Is she a close friend of yours?

NORA. Yes, but what does that –

KROGSTAD. I used to know her too.

NORA. I'm aware.

KROGSTAD. Oh, you know about that. Thought you might. Anyway, my question for you is very simple – is Mrs. Linde getting a job at the Savings Bank?

NORA. It's completely out of line for you to ask me that, you do realize, as one of my husband's employees. But I'll tell you anyway – yes, Torvald gave Kristine a job. Because I asked him to.

KROGSTAD. I suspected that.

NORA. I have a little bit of influence, as it turns out. Being a woman doesn't always mean that – you know, when you're in a subordinate position, you should be careful around people who, um –

KROGSTAD. Who have influence.

NORA. Exactly.

KROGSTAD. *(A change of tone.)* Would you be so kind…as to use your influence on my behalf?

NORA. What are you talking about?

KROGSTAD. Would you please ensure that I keep my – "subordinate position," as you called it, at the bank?

NORA. Is someone trying to take your job away?

KROGSTAD. Don't play innocent, Mrs. Helmer. I'm sure your friend doesn't want to worry about bumping into me at the office, and I can guess she's also the reason I was pushed out the door just now –

NORA. But that has nothing to do with –

KROGSTAD. All right, anyway – there's still time for you to use your influence to keep me in my job.

NORA. But – I don't really have any influence...

KROGSTAD. Really? You were just saying –

NORA. Obviously I didn't mean it like *that*. You think I have that kind of influence over my husband?

KROGSTAD. I've known your husband since high school, I believe he can be swayed.

NORA. Are you being rude now? The door is right over there.

KROGSTAD. Feisty!

NORA. I'm not afraid of you. In the new year our business together will be over.

KROGSTAD. *(Controlled.)* Listen. I'm prepared to do anything to keep my job at the bank.

NORA. I can see that.

KROGSTAD. It's not just for the money – that's the least of it, actually. You probably know, since everyone seems to, that a long time ago I committed an...indiscretion.

NORA. I heard something about it.

KROGSTAD. It never went to court, but that didn't matter, it was like every door was closed to me from then on. So I started doing the business you know about. I didn't have much choice, and I've been fairer than most. But my sons are growing up now and I owe it to them to win back some respect for our family. That job at the bank...it was like the first rung on the ladder. And now your husband wants to kick me off the ladder back into the dirt.

NORA. But honestly, it just isn't in my power to help you.

KROGSTAD. Because you don't want to. But if I had to, I could force you.

(Pause.)

NORA. You wouldn't tell my husband that I owe you money.

(He doesn't answer, lets her consider the possibility.)

That would be a shameful thing to do.

(Almost in tears.)

That you would take my secret, which I'm so proud of, and tell him in such an ugly, nasty way – that he would hear it from *you*. That would be...just incredibly... unpleasant.

KROGSTAD. Unpleasant? That's all?

NORA. Go ahead, do it; Torvald will see what a terrible person you are and then he'll definitely fire you.

KROGSTAD. I asked you a question. Is a little "unpleasantness" at home all you're afraid of?

NORA. He'll just pay the rest of what we owe and then we won't have anything more to do with you.

KROGSTAD. Listen, Mrs. Helmer – I can't tell whether your memory isn't very good or you really don't understand what's at stake here. I think I have to explain a few things.

NORA. What things?

KROGSTAD. When you came to me to borrow money, I said I'd find it for you on a few conditions. You were so preoccupied with your husband's health that you might have missed some of the details, so let me remind you of them. I wrote up a promissory note –

NORA. Which I signed.

KROGSTAD. Right. And below your signature were some lines for a guarantor, which your father was supposed to sign –

NORA. And he did, what is / this –?

KROGSTAD. The date was blank, so your father could sign and date it. You remember that?

NORA. Vaguely.

KROGSTAD. I gave you the promissory note to mail to your father. Sound right?

NORA. Yes?

KROGSTAD. Which you must have done immediately because five or six days later you brought it back to me with his signature. And I paid you the full amount.

NORA. And I've been keeping up with the payments, haven't I?

KROGSTAD. Mostly. But to get back to the subject – that was a hard time for you, I imagine.

NORA. Very hard.

KROGSTAD. Your father was also sick, if I remember.

NORA. He was dying.

KROGSTAD. He passed soon after that?

NORA. Yes.

KROGSTAD. Happen to remember the date?

NORA. Papa died on September 29th.

KROGSTAD. That's right, I looked it up. And so we have a little problem...that I can't seem to work out.

NORA. What problem? Where is this –

KROGSTAD. The problem, you see, is that your father signed the note three days after he died.

NORA. That's impossible –

KROGSTAD. Your father died on September 29th. But he dated his signature October 2nd. Isn't that puzzling?

(**NORA** *is silent.*)

Can you explain it?

(*Still silent.*)

It's also striking that the date isn't in your father's handwriting, though the penmanship does look familiar to me. But that's okay, your father might've forgotten to date his signature and then someone else did it before hearing that he'd died, nothing illegal about that. What matters is the signature itself. And that's genuine, right? Your father did sign his own name?

(*A pause.* **NORA** *is overtaken by defiance.*)

NORA. No, he didn't. I signed his name.

KROGSTAD. I'm not sure you realize what a dangerous confession you've just made.

NORA. Why? You'll get the rest of your money soon.

KROGSTAD. I have to ask, why didn't you just send it to your father?

NORA. He was so sick! I couldn't ask him to guarantee the money without telling him what it was for, but I couldn't tell him that Torvald's life was in danger while he was lying there dying –

KROGSTAD. Maybe you should've canceled your trip.

NORA. I couldn't do that, the trip was to save Torvald's life.

KROGSTAD. But didn't it occur to you that you were defrauding me?

NORA. I really wasn't thinking about you at all. You were driving me out of my mind, making it so complicated for me to get the loan when you knew how sick my husband was.

KROGSTAD. You have absolutely no idea what you're guilty of, do you? I think I should tell you that it's more or less the same crime I committed years ago, the one that ruined my reputation and my life.

NORA. What? Are you trying to tell me you did something noble to save your wife?

KROGSTAD. The law is not interested in motives.

NORA. Then the law is stupid.

KROGSTAD. That may be, but if I bring this contract to court, the law is what they'll use to judge you.

NORA. That can't be right. A daughter doesn't have the right to prevent her dying father from worrying? A wife doesn't have the right to save her husband's life? I may not be an expert on the law, but I'm pretty sure there are allowances for those kinds of situations. And you're a lawyer, shouldn't you know this? You must be a lousy lawyer.

KROGSTAD. It's possible. But the kind of business we have together – you're aware I do know a good deal about that. Right?

(Off her troubled expression.)

Good. You'll make your own decision. But I'll tell you this…if I'm thrown back into the dirt? You're coming with me.

(He exits.)

*(**NORA** is still for a while, frightened, not sure what to believe.)*

*(**IVAR** appears in the doorway.)*

IVAR. Can we play now that the man is gone?

NORA. *(Startled.)* Sweetheart – listen! Let's not tell anyone about the man, okay, not even Daddy. Shhhh, it's our special secret!

IVAR. Can we play?

NORA. Not now.

IVAR. But you said –

NORA. *(Snapping.)* I know I did but I can't now.

(More gently.)

Go back to Anne-Marie. Go ahead, sweetheart…

(He goes.)

Oh God.

*(**TORVALD** enters.)*

TORVALD. Hi.

NORA. Oh – you're already back.

TORVALD. Did anyone come by?

NORA. Here? No.

TORVALD. That's strange. I saw Krogstad walk out the front door.

NORA. Oh! Right, Krogstad was here for a minute.

TORVALD. Nora. It's written all over your face – he was asking you to put in a good word for him.

NORA. Yes.

TORVALD. And pretend it was your own idea? You were going to hide it from me that he was here.

NORA. Yes, but –

TORVALD. Nora, what were you thinking? Making promises to a man like that? And then lying to me?

NORA. Lying?

TORVALD. Didn't you say no one came by?

TORVALD. No more lies in that pretty mouth, okay? You're my songbird, no false notes. All right, let's not talk about it any more.

NORA. Torvald?

TORVALD. Hm?

NORA. I'm excited for Thursday night.

TORVALD. What's Thursday night?

NORA. The costume party at The Stenborgs.

TORVALD. Mm, I can't wait to see what you come up with to surprise me.

NORA. I can't think of a good costume, every idea I've had is so obvious.

TORVALD. Is that how my baby's feeling about it?

NORA. What are all those papers?

TORVALD. Bank business.

NORA. Already?

TORVALD. I convinced the board to let me make some personnel changes over the holiday so that I can start fresh in the New Year.

NORA. So that's why Krogstad –

TORVALD. Mm-hm.

NORA. If you weren't so busy I'd ask you for a giant favor.

TORVALD. What kind of favor?

NORA. You have the best taste. Can't you choose my costume for the party?

TORVALD. Oh, so my headstrong little bird needs some help after all?

NORA. Desperately.

TORVALD. I'll think about it.

NORA. Thank you.

So is it really so bad, whatever Krogstad did?

TORVALD. He forged signatures. Do you know what that means?

NORA. Well...maybe he did it out of need, or –

TORVALD. Sure, or maybe it was just a moment of recklessness. I would never condemn a man unequivocally for one mistake –

NORA. Right, I agree!

TORVALD. At least not if he came clean and accepted his punishment.

NORA. Punishment?

TORVALD. But Krogstad didn't do that; he squirmed out of it like a coward and that's why he's beyond redemption.

NORA. Do you really think he's –

TORVALD. Imagine how much deception there is in his daily life, even with his own family, his wife and children – the children, that's the worst part.

NORA. Why?

TORVALD. Because it's a sick atmosphere, the lies contaminate the entire home. Every breath those children take in that house is filled with...evil...spores.

NORA. Isn't that a little...?

TORVALD. Believe me, in my line of work I've learned more about criminals than I ever wanted to know. Basically every one of them had a deceitful mother.

NORA. Why just the mother?

TORVALD. It's usually the mother, but the father does have some effect too. Krogstad knows all this as well as I do, as a lawyer himself, but still he chose to poison his children with lies and excuses.

(He reaches out to **NORA**.*)*

TORVALD. And that's why my little bird has to promise not to take his side anymore. Shake on it. Hey. Give me your hand.

(She does.)

All better. Anyway, I could never have worked with that man, I literally feel sick around people like that.

(She pulls her hand away.)

NORA. It's hot in here. And now I'm so behind getting ready for tonight…

TORVALD. I'll get some work done before dinner. And I'll mull over your costume, okay? Also…I might have a little something for you to wrap in gold paper and hang on the tree.

(He touches her.)

Don't worry, I'm not angry at you. Pure heart.

(He exits. **NORA** *stares dully.)*

(**ANNE-MARIE** *comes in.)*

ANNE-MARIE. The little ones keep asking to see you.

NORA. They can't come in here. You stay with them, Anne-Marie.

ANNE-MARIE. *(Thrown.)* All right…

(**ANNE-MARIE** *leaves.)*

NORA. Poison my children? No…it's not possible. It can't be…

End of Act One

ACT TWO

(**NORA** *thinks she hears something from the hall; she listens.*)

(*Nothing.*)

(*She shakes her head, annoyed with herself.*)

NORA. Of course no one's there…

(*But then she thinks she hears something again – a creak on the stairs. She looks. Sees nothing.*)

(**ANNE-MARIE** *enters.*)

ANNE-MARIE. Well I found the – Nora?

NORA. Yes?

ANNE-MARIE. Not going out again?

NORA. Just checking the mailbox.

ANNE-MARIE. It's Christmas day, I don't think you'll get any mail.

NORA. No, you're right.

ANNE-MARIE. I finally found your costume, it's not in great shape –

NORA. Maybe I'll just tear it to shreds.

ANNE-MARIE. Silly! It can be fixed.

NORA. I'll go ask Kristine if she can help me.

ANNE-MARIE. If you keep running in and out in this nasty weather you'll get yourself sick.

NORA. I wouldn't mind that. How are the children?

(**ANNE-MARIE** *looks at* **NORA**, *then says discreetly:*)

ANNE-MARIE. Playing with their Christmas presents.

NORA. Are they still asking for me?

ANNE-MARIE. Of course they are. They're so used to being with you. How much longer do you think –?

NORA. I don't know; for now I can't be with them as much as before.

(**ANNE-MARIE** *wants to ask more, but holds her tongue.)*

ANNE-MARIE. Well. Children can get used to anything, I guess.

NORA. Do you think so? Would they get used to it if I disappeared forever?

ANNE-MARIE. Now what in the world / are you –

NORA. I've always wanted to ask you, Anne-Marie – how could you bear to give away your daughter to strangers?

ANNE-MARIE. It was what I had to do, to become your nanny.

NORA. But was that what you wanted?

ANNE-MARIE. I was lucky to get that job. A poor girl like me, who'd gotten in trouble? And the baby's father took off...no, I was very lucky, and I knew it.

NORA. Do you think your daughter has forgotten you?

ANNE-MARIE. Oh no, I know she hasn't. She sent me a card when she was confirmed, and another when she got married.

NORA. You were a good mother to me, Anne-Marie.

ANNE-MARIE. Poor little Nora, I was the only mother you had.

NORA. And I know if my children needed you to...

ANNE-MARIE. To what? Sweetheart...

NORA. Don't listen to me. You should get back to them. I better...I'll get the costume all fixed, you'll see, it'll be lovely again for tomorrow.

ANNE-MARIE. You'll be the prettiest one there.

>   (**ANNE-MARIE** *exits.*)

>   (**NORA** *waits till she's gone, then makes a move to leave –*)

>   (*And immediately stops herself.*)

NORA. (*Under her breath.*) Stupid. Where am I going?

>   (*She stands still for a moment, trying to figure out what to do.*)

Stop thinking about it. Just stop thinking about it.

>   (*She takes a breath.*)

Just check the mailbox one –

>   (*Shift.* **KRISTINE** *appears –* **NORA** *shrieks and* **KRISTINE** *startles.*)

Sorry! Come in. It's just you, right? I'm so glad you're here.

KRISTINE. I heard you came by looking for me.

NORA. Yes, I was in your neighborhood, um...oh, I need your help! Did I tell you we're going to a costume party tomorrow?

KRISTINE. No.

NORA. We are, our upstairs neighbors – he's an ambassador – anyway, Torvald wants me to go as a Neapolitan fisher girl and do this dance I learned years ago in Capri –

KRISTINE. What? You're going to perform?

NORA. Torvald thinks I should. He had a costume made for me back then but it's falling apart and I don't know if I can –

KRISTINE. Oh I'll fix it up for you, it can't be that bad.

NORA. Thank you, you're so sweet.

KRISTINE. Can I come by tomorrow and see you in costume before you go?

NORA. Of course.

KRISTINE. I'm sorry, I haven't even thanked you for last night, it was a lovely evening.

NORA. I'm glad you thought so, it wasn't our best dinner party. I wish you'd come to town a little sooner. But yes, Torvald's an excellent host.

KRISTINE. You're not so bad either; you're your father's daughter. I wanted to ask, is Dr. Rank always like that?

NORA. Like what?

KRISTINE. Depressed.

NORA. Oh – yes, but yesterday was worse than usual. He's very sick, unfortunately, and the illness has started to affect his spine. His father...had affairs, that's a nice way of putting it, so Dr. Rank has been sick since birth.

(**KRISTINE** *stares.*)

What?

KRISTINE. You certainly know a lot about him. Does Dr. Rank visit every day?

NORA. Always. He's Torvald's oldest friend and he and I are very close, too. He's part of the family.

KRISTINE. But can you trust him? He seems like a flatterer.

NORA. What? No, he's definitely not that, why?

KRISTINE. Yesterday when you introduced me he said he had heard all about me, but then when I met your husband I could tell he had no idea who I was. So how could Dr. Rank –

NORA. *(Laughing.)* No, that's all true. Torvald's very jealous, which is so sweet – he doesn't like to share me and he used to get upset when I talked about missing my old friends from home, so I stopped. But I talk to Peter about it all the time, he likes to hear about my old life.

KRISTINE. Nora, I'm a little older than you, and I have a lot more experience, so please listen to me when I say – you have to get out of this situation, with Dr. Rank.

NORA. What "situation"?

KRISTINE. Yesterday you were talking about a rich older man, who would give you money –

NORA. Right, an imaginary one –

KRISTINE. Nora – do you really think I haven't guessed who loaned you all that money?

(**NORA** *bursts out laughing.*)

NORA. You think I secretly borrowed from my husband's best friend, who's here every day? That would be… incredibly awkward.

KRISTINE. You swear it wasn't him?

NORA. That never even occurred to me. Anyway, he didn't have the money back then, he inherited it later.

KRISTINE. That was probably for the best.

NORA. No, I would never ask him.

>   *(A new thought.)*

If I did, I'm sure he would –

KRISTINE. But you won't.

NORA. No. No.

>   *(A beat.)*

Though it's true that if I told him –

KRISTINE. Behind Torvald's back?

NORA. Well it's already behind his back, this stupid loan, and I have to get out of it. I have to.

KRISTINE. I agree, but you also have to tell your –

NORA. Once you pay off a loan you get your promissory note back, right?

KRISTINE. I believe so.

NORA. And then you can tear it up or burn it or whatever you want –?

KRISTINE. What's going on with you? You're hiding something from me.

>   *(**NORA** looks at her fearfully.)*

NORA. You can tell that just by looking at me?

KRISTINE. What happened since we talked yesterday? Tell me.

>   *(**NORA** hears something.)*

NORA. Torvald's coming. Anne-Marie has my costume in the playroom – Torvald hates seeing sewing around – go in there, Anne-Marie will get you a needle and thread.

KRISTINE. Fine, but I'm not leaving until you tell me what's going on.

(**KRISTINE** *exits as* **TORVALD** *enters.*)

NORA. I'm so glad you're home.

TORVALD. Who was that?

NORA. Kristine, she's helping fix my costume so I'll look perfect tomorrow night.

TORVALD. That was a pretty good idea I had, huh? I'd say I came through for you.

NORA. And I very graciously agreed to indulge you, didn't I?

(*He laughs.*)

TORVALD. "Indulge me"? That's hilarious. You asked for my help.

NORA. I –

TORVALD. That's okay, you little lunatic, I know what you meant. All right, I'll leave you to your sewing and trying-on…

NORA. You have a lot of work?

TORVALD. Tons. I just came from the bank.

(*He starts to exit.*)

NORA. Torvald?

(*He turns back.*)

What if your little bird asked you for something? Would you do it?

TORVALD. I'd have to know what it is first.

NORA. The little bird would run around and play and sing all over the house –

TORVALD. She does that anyway.

NORA. I'll pretend to be a fairy and dance for you in the moonlight. Remember how we used to –

TORVALD. Is this about Krogstad?

NORA. Please, Torvald, I'm begging you –

TORVALD. You're actually bringing that up to me again.

NORA. Just do what I'm asking, let him keep his job –

TORVALD. I already gave his job away, Nora. To your friend, because you asked me to –

NORA. And I'm so grateful. But couldn't you fire someone else instead –?

TORVALD. Because you weren't thinking and made him a promise you should never, ever have made? You shouldn't even have been talking to him, and now you expect me to / clean up your –

NORA. But that's not why, he has a big mouth, you told me that, he'll spread nasty rumors about you and it could really hurt us, Torvald. I'm so afraid of him...

(**TORVALD** *softens a bit.*)

TORVALD. I see. This is bringing up bad memories, huh?

NORA. What do you mean?

TORVALD. You're thinking about your father.

(**NORA** *hadn't been, but she grasps onto this.*)

NORA. Yes! Remember how vicious people were, and it ended up in the papers? He would have been fired from the civil service if anyone other than you had been sent to investigate him. And you were so kind and helpful, otherwise it would have been a disaster...

TORVALD. What you're forgetting, baby, is that I'm nothing like your father. He was not...let's say, above reproach. I am. And I intend to stay that way.

NORA. But who knows what that awful man could come up with to attack you…and just when we're so close to complete happiness – think of the children, Torvald, I'm begging you –

TORVALD. Even if I wanted to keep him, your pleading like this would make it impossible. Everyone at the bank already knows I'm planning to fire him, imagine if word got around that the bank manager's *wife* is the one calling the shots –

NORA. Would that be so terrible?

TORVALD. No, no it would be fine. If before my official first day leading this company I was already seen as spineless, weak, susceptible to outside influence. Is that what you want? Because the most important thing, obviously, is that you get your way.

NORA. But Torvald –

TORVALD. Listen, there's another reason I haven't even told you that I can't under any circumstances have Krogstad working under me.

NORA. What is it?

TORVALD. I could overlook his moral failings if I absolutely had to.

NORA. I know you could, because you're so kind –

TORVALD. And I've heard he's actually very good at his work. But we went to school together, we became friends – I don't know what I was thinking, I was young, and I immediately regretted it, but anyway – he, uh. Some people back then called me by a nickname, and he – he still uses it, even in front of other people, I mean he uses it every chance he gets, it's a power play, he just loves bursting out with "Torvey this" and "Torvey that" and it's mortifying. I can't have that when I'm establishing myself at the bank.

NORA. But Torvald. You're kidding, right?

TORVALD. No, why?

NORA. That just seems so...petty.

TORVALD. Petty? Oh I'm petty. I see.

NORA. *You're* not petty at all, which is why this seems –

TORVALD. No, I'm being petty, so I must be petty.

NORA. Torvald, I didn't / say that –

TORVALD. Yes you did. And I'm getting tired of this conversation.

NORA. Where are you going?

Torvald. Torvald!

> *(Shift.)*

What have you done?

TORVALD. He's fired.

NORA. Go take it back. It's not too late.

Torvald, please. Please, for me. And for yourself. And for our family.

> *(He doesn't respond.)*

Then I'll go –

> *(She makes a move; gently but firmly, he stops her, holds her there.)*

You have no idea what you're doing to us.

TORVALD. It's done. It's over. Breathe.

> *(He holds her.)*

NORA. Oh, God...

TORVALD. It's okay. I forgive you.

> *(She reacts. Forgives her for what? Does he know?)*

I forgive you even though this behavior is really insulting.

(She's about to protest.)

You really think I have anything to fear from that guy? You think someone like him has any power over someone like me?

NORA. But –

TORVALD. It's okay, I know you're only acting like this because you love me. And that's sweet, it's very touching. Baby, you're trembling. Shhhhhh. Listen, whatever happens, I can handle it. And when we're up against a real crisis, you'll see how strong I can be. I'll do anything for you.

NORA. What do you mean?

TORVALD. Exactly what I said.

NORA. *(Composed.)* You'll never have to do that.

TORVALD. Okay, we'll share it. That's exactly how it should be.

Feeling better now? You got yourself all worked up there.

You better practice your dance. I'll keep my door closed, don't worry about bothering me.

(He hesitates another moment, then goes to his study.)

When Rank comes, send him right in.

(He exits.)

NORA. *(To herself.)* He'd really do it. I can't let him.

No...I need a way out.

(The doorbell rings, a long-ish ring.)

Peter.

        (She stands, staring, as if deciding something.
        Then – Shift. **RANK** *is before her.)*

NORA. I recognized the way you rang the doorbell.

        (She smiles at him. He smiles back.)

Torvald's busy, unfortunately.

RANK. What about you?

NORA. You know I always have time for you.

RANK. I'll take you up on that for as long as I can.

NORA. What does that mean?

RANK. Am I scaring you?

NORA. You're being a little mysterious, that's all. Is something about to happen?

RANK. I'm afraid so. I didn't think it would be quite so soon.

NORA. *(Alarmed.)* What do you know? Tell me.

RANK. Things are going downhill fast with me.

NORA. *(Relieved.)* With you?

RANK. I'm the sickest of all my patients. I've been in denial, I guess. But these last few days I've taken a good hard look at myself, and...in the next few months I'll be worm food.

NORA. Stop! You don't have to say it in such an ugly way.

RANK. Well it's an ugly thing. I have to conduct one more test, then I should know more or less when the disintegration begins. I have to tell you something. We both know our dear delicate Torvald doesn't have the stomach for anything this nasty. I don't want him visiting me when I'm sick –

NORA. But –

RANK. I don't want him to come, period. Once I get the results of this test, if it's what I suspect, I'll send my business card to you with a black X over it, that way you'll know the decay has begun.

NORA. Ugh, that's so depressing. I was hoping you'd be in a good mood today.

RANK. Staring down my death? That's a lot to ask. And I'm suffering for someone else's sins, does that seem fair to you?

NORA. Please, I can't take it, cheer up –

RANK. You're right. It is actually kind of funny, to think my poor, innocent spine is paying for my father's rowdy army days.

NORA. *(Hint of mischief.)* He ate too much foie gras, you mean, right?

RANK. *(Same.)* Far too much. And truffles.

NORA. Truffles, mm. Oysters, too, I think I heard.

RANK. Oh oysters. So many oysters.

NORA. And all that champagne. It's a shame that all those delicious things affect the spine.

RANK. Well, especially if that spine's unfortunate owner hasn't, um…tasted them.

NORA. Yes. That is so sad.

(He looks at her searchingly.)

Why are you smiling?

RANK. Why are you laughing?

NORA. Because you smiled. Stop!

RANK. You're bad.

NORA. I'm in a crazy mood, watch out.

RANK. *(Thrilled.)* I will.

NORA. You. Cannot. Die on us.

RANK. You'll get over it. Out of sight, out of mind.

(This thought strikes fear in her.)

NORA. Do you think that's true?

RANK. You find someone new, and then –

NORA. Who finds someone new?

RANK. You and Torvald will, when I'm gone. In fact I think that's already underway. Tell me more about your friend Mrs. Linde.

NORA. You're not jealous of Kristine?

RANK. Yes I am. She'll take my place in this house, you'll see –

NORA. Don't talk so loudly, she's in there.

RANK. Oh, so she's back today!

NORA. She's just helping with my costume, you're being impossible! Snap out of it, think of something happy. Tomorrow I'll be all dressed up, and I'll dance, and you have to imagine that I'm doing it just for you. I mean for Torvald, too, obviously, but...hey.

RANK. What?

NORA. Do you know what I'll be wearing tomorrow? Your favorite...

RANK. ...silk stockings?

NORA. The color of my skin.

RANK. Hmmmm...

NORA. What? You don't think they'll still fit?

RANK. I'd need a little more information to make a judgment like that.

NORA. You dirty old man.

RANK. What else will I see tomorrow?

NORA. I'm not telling you any more because you're misbehaving.

> *(A pause.)*

RANK. When we sit together like this, just you and me, I start to think…I don't know what would have happened to me if I had never come to this house.

NORA. I'm glad you're happy here with us.

RANK. I hate to leave you –

NORA. Stop, you're not leaving us –

RANK. I wish there were some way to thank you, something I could leave you, other than…empty space for someone else to fill.

NORA. Well, what if there was something…never mind.

RANK. No, what?

NORA. It's…it's big, it's too much to ask.

RANK. Ask me.

NORA. I can't.

RANK. Ask, you'll make me so happy –

NORA. You don't even know what it is.

RANK. Then tell me. Don't you trust me?

NORA. You know I do, more than anyone else in the world. You're my truest friend. Peter…

> *(He listens, leans toward her as she leans toward him.)*

I need your help preventing something from happening. It's about Torvald. You know how much he loves me; if he had to, he would give up his life for me.

RANK. Nora…he's not the only one.

NORA. *(Jolted.)* What?

    (A mortifying pause.)

RANK. You didn't hear me?

NORA. *(Sadly.)* No, I...I did.

RANK. I've wanted to tell you for a long time, and...this might be my last chance. So now you know. And you also know that you can tell me anything, and ask me anything –

    (NORA *moves away.)*

Nora –

NORA. That was really wrong of you, Peter.

RANK. What? Falling in love with you?

NORA. No, telling me about it! That was unnecessary.

RANK. Are you saying you knew?

    (She doesn't answer.)

Nora, did you know?

NORA. How am I supposed to know what I knew and didn't know? I have no idea. Why did you have to pick this moment to ruin everything?

RANK. Well...anyway, you know that I'm here for you, body and soul. So what do you need from me?

NORA. Nothing.

RANK. Tell me.

NORA. After that? No thanks.

RANK. Okay, slap me on the wrist, and then let me help you. Please.

NORA. I don't need any help, it was just my imagination. I have an over-active imagination, right? That's all it was.

(She smiles coldly at him.)

Classy. Are you ashamed of yourself yet?

RANK. No, I'm not. But if you want me to leave and stay away –

NORA. You'll keep coming here as usual, you know Torvald needs you.

RANK. What about you?

NORA. Oh, I always have a great time when you're here.

RANK. Maybe that's what confused me. Sometimes I got the feeling you liked being with me as much as your husband, maybe more.

NORA. Well there are the people you love most and the people you'd rather spend time with.

RANK. Hm. True.

NORA. Growing up, I obviously loved Papa best, but I was always sneaking down to be with the maids, because they were fun and they didn't tell me what to do.

RANK. So in this analogy, I'm the maids.

NORA. *(Remorsefully.)* I didn't mean it that way. But you can see how being with Torvald is a lot like being with Papa –

> *(**ANNE-MARIE** enters, whispers something to **NORA**.)*

Oh...

RANK. Something wrong?

NORA. No, it's just – it's my new costume –

RANK. I thought Mrs. Linde was sewing your costume.

NORA. This is a different one I ordered – don't tell Torvald –

RANK. Aha. So that's the secret.

NORA. Yes. He's in his office, go distract him for a while.

RANK. You can count on me.

(*He goes.* **NORA** *turns to* **ANNE-MARIE.**)

NORA. He's in the kitchen?

ANNE-MARIE. He said he wouldn't leave without speaking to you.

NORA. Fine. He can come in. But Anne-Marie – don't mention it to anyone, it's a surprise for my husband.

(**ANNE-MARIE** *nods and exits.*)

(**KROGSTAD** *enters.*)

Keep your voice down, my husband's in there.

KROGSTAD. So?

NORA. What do you want?

KROGSTAD. I suppose you know that I've been fired.

NORA. I did everything I could to stop it, I swear.

KROGSTAD. How could your husband do that to you? He knows the threat I pose to you and he still –

NORA. He doesn't know.

KROGSTAD. Okay, that makes more sense. I wouldn't expect this display of principled courage from Torvey –

NORA. Don't you dare disrespect him.

KROGSTAD. Excuse me, all due respect. But since you're going to these lengths to keep it a secret, I gather you've learned a little more about the seriousness of what you've done.

NORA. What is it you came here for?

KROGSTAD. Actually, I wanted to see how you're doing. I may be a crooked loan shark but I do have a heart, you know.

NORA. Then show it. Think about my children.

KROGSTAD. Did you and your husband think about mine? Forget it– I just wanted to tell you not to worry too much. I'm not going to do anything right now.

NORA. Really? I appreciate that.

KROGSTAD. We can deal with this calmly, like adults. No one other than the three of us needs to find out about it.

NORA. My husband can never find out.

KROGSTAD. How are you planning to prevent it? Can you pay the rest of what you owe?

NORA. Not right this second, but –

KROGSTAD. You have some other way to raise the money?

NORA. No – or, not that I want to use.

KROGSTAD. It doesn't matter anyway. If you had the cash today, I still wouldn't give you the promissory note back.

NORA. What are you going to do with it?

KROGSTAD. Just keep it. Have it with me. I won't tell anyone else about it. So in case you're thinking of doing something desperate –

(She looks at him – can he see that in her eyes?)

Like running away, or something worse – let it go. Forget about it.

NORA. How did you know I was thinking about that?

KROGSTAD. I thought of it too. Personally, though, I didn't have the guts.

NORA. Neither do I.

KROGSTAD. *(Relieved.)* Okay. Good, so you don't either, right?

NORA. No. I don't.

KROGSTAD. It would be incredibly stupid. I have a letter here for your husband.

NORA. That tells him everything?

KROGSTAD. As sensitively as possible.

NORA. *(Suddenly frantic.)* Tear it up. I'll find a way to get the money.

KROGSTAD. But I just told you –

NORA. No, not the just the money I owe you, whatever you want. You were going to demand money from Torvald, right? So tell me how much and I'll get it for you.

KROGSTAD. I wasn't going to demand money from anyone.

NORA. Then what is it you want?

KROGSTAD. To get back on my feet. I want some dignity. For the last year I've been scrupulous, no mistakes, no shortcuts, my family's been living on nothing but that was okay, I was willing to be patient and work my way back up. Now I'm being pushed down again and this time I'm not gonna take it. I want to come back to the bank, but not in the same job. Torvald will have to promote me.

NORA. He won't do it.

KROGSTAD. Sure he will. I know him, he'll be too scared not to. And then you'll see, in a few years I'll be running the bank, not him.

NORA. I'll never let that happen.

KROGSTAD. No? What will you –

NORA. Now I have the courage.

KROGSTAD. Don't fool yourself, you've been spoiled your whole life.

NORA. You'll see.

KROGSTAD. Under the ice, is that what you're thinking? Float up in the spring, bloated, hideous, your hair fallen out –

NORA. You don't scare me.

KROGSTAD. You don't scare me. And it wouldn't do any good anyway, Torvey would still be in my pocket.

NORA. You mean even if I was…

KROGSTAD. Then I'd have total control over how you're remembered. Right?

(She stares at him, speechless.)

Okay, now I think you understand. So don't do anything reckless. I'll leave your husband this letter now and I'll be waiting for his reply. And remember – he's the one who made me do this. I'll never forgive him for that.

*(He exits. **NORA** stands stock still, in shocked silence.)*

*(**KRISTINE** enters.)*

KRISTINE. I think I've fixed every tear. Do you want to try it – what's wrong?

NORA. Kristine, can you go out in the hall and look in our mailbox? The top is glass, you should be able to see whether there's a letter…

*(Puzzled, **KRISTINE** goes and comes back.)*

KRISTINE. Yes, there is. It's from Krogstad.

NORA. That's it. I'm lost.

KRISTINE. So he lent you the money.

NORA. Yes. And now he's telling Torvald everything.

KRISTINE. Oh, Nora. It might be hard to see it now, but I think it's for the best.

NORA. I haven't told you everything. I forged a signature.

KRISTINE. You what?

NORA. And now I need to tell you, so you're my witness. In case I lose my mind, and I might –

KRISTINE. Nora!

NORA. Or if something happens to me, so I can't be here anymore –

KRISTINE. Honey –

NORA. If someone tries to take the blame for me, then you're my witness that it's not true. I'm not crazy, I've never been so clear about anything: no one else knew about it. I did it by myself. Remember that.

KRISTINE. I will. But I don't understand –

NORA. Of course not, how could you? The most beautiful thing is about to happen.

KRISTINE. The most beautiful...?

NORA. Yes, and horrible. It's absolutely awful, and we have to stop it from happening.

KRISTINE. I'll go talk to Krogstad –

NORA. Don't, he'll hurt you!

KRISTINE. No he won't. He used to be in love with me.

NORA. Him?

KRISTINE. Where does he live?

NORA. I don't know.

KRISTINE. The letter...

(**KRISTINE** *goes back to the letter box.*)

TORVALD. (*Offstage.*) Nora!

(**NORA** *gasps.*)

NORA. What is it?

TORVALD. *(Offstage.)* I didn't mean to scare you – you locked the door! Can I come out?

NORA. No, I –

(**KRISTINE** *comes back in.*)

TORVALD. *(Offstage.)* Are you trying on your costume?

NORA. Yes! Kristine did such a lovely job, I'm going to be so pretty for you, Torvald!

KRISTINE. He lives around the corner.

NORA. But it doesn't matter, the letter is already in the box, and Torvald keeps the only key.

KRISTINE. Then Krogstad has to ask for it back, we'll think up some excuse –

NORA. But this is the time Torvald usually checks the mail.

KRISTINE. Hold him off, I'll be back as soon as I can.

(**KRISTINE** *exits.* **NORA** *unlocks the door to the office, collects herself.*)

NORA. You can come in now.

TORVALD. Oh, am I allowed in my own living room again? So kind of you...

(*He enters with* **RANK** *and looks at her.*)

What's going on?

NORA. What do you mean?

TORVALD. Rank led me to believe I was going to be treated to some exciting costume scenario –

RANK. I thought so, apparently I had that wrong.

NORA. No one sees me in costume until tomorrow night, sorry, gentlemen.

TORVALD. You look exhausted. Have you been practicing too hard?

NORA. I haven't practiced at all.

TORVALD. You'll need to.

NORA. I need your help, I've forgotten everything.

TORVALD. It'll come back, we'll take a look at it.

NORA. Yes, can you please take charge, Torvald? I'm so nervous; promise me you won't do anything other than rehearse with me tonight. No work, no papers, nothing. Please? Promise?

TORVALD. Tonight, I'm all yours. Hey, it's okay. I'm here. Let me just check one thing –

NORA. Where are you going?

TORVALD. Mailbox.

NORA. Don't! There's nothing there.

TORVALD. I'll just check anyway.

(He's about to walk out the door.)

NORA. Wait! I can't perform tomorrow if I don't rehearse with you.

TORVALD. Are you really that nervous?

NORA. Unbearably. There's time to rehearse before dinner, come on. Direct me, like you always do.

TORVALD. Okay, at your service.

*(**NORA** begins to beat out a rhythm.)*

NORA. Clap!

*(**TORVALD** and **RANK** clap to the rhythm as **NORA** starts to dance.)*

TORVALD. Slow down, you're ahead.

NORA. I can't help it.

TORVALD. A little less violently.

NORA. I can't. It has to be like this.

TORVALD. Stop!

> *(She does.)*

Listen.

> *(He starts to clap again, setting the beat slower. **RANK** joins. She starts to dance.)*

Not yet, just listen first, feel the rhythm.

> *(She closes her eyes, trying to follow his instructions, but breaks out dancing.)*

Wait, slow down…

> *(**NORA** dances more and more wildly. **TORVALD** stops clapping, leaving the beat to **RANK**, as he attempts to tame **NORA** – she takes no notice.)*

Easy, easy. Easy!

> *(**KRISTINE** enters, stares.)*

KRISTINE. Oh –

NORA. Kristine! Look at me!

TORVALD. Nora, this is not life or death!

NORA. *(Biting his head off.)* Yes it is!

TORVALD. *(To **RANK** who is still clapping.)* Stop.

> *(Even with no beat, **NORA** keeps dancing, ever wilder. Like an external force is thrashing her body around.)*

TORVALD. Stop, stop, stop, stop, stop!

(He puts his arms around her, subduing her. She finally stops.)

(She catches her breath.)

Well. You certainly need a lot of rehearsal.

NORA. You see? Promise me you won't leave my side.

TORVALD. I do, I promise.

NORA. And you can't think of anyone else either, only me. You can't open any letters, or look in the mailbox –

TORVALD. You're still afraid of that man.

NORA. Yes, but that's not –

TORVALD. There's already a letter from him in the box. Isn't there?

NORA. I don't know. I think so. Please don't let anything come between us, just until tomorrow night. I'm begging you.

RANK. *(Quietly.)* Just do what she says, man.

TORVALD. You win, you little nut.

(He kisses her.)

But after you dance tomorrow –

NORA. Then you'll be free.

(ANNE-MARIE enters.)

ANNE-MARIE. Excuse me, dinner's ready.

NORA. Bring out some champagne, Torvald.

(ANNE-MARIE exits.)

TORVALD. Oh really, is it going to be that kind of party?

NORA. And chocolate cake!

TORVALD. Shhh, you're all worked up. Be my sweet baby bird again, okay?

NORA. I will. You two go ahead – Kristine, will you help me fix my hair?

RANK. *(Subdued, as they leave.)* Could she be, uh… [pregnant]

TORVALD. What? No, it's just that neurotic fear I told you about.

>(**TORVALD** *and* **RANK** *exit.* **NORA** *turns to* **KRISTINE.***)*

NORA. So?

KRISTINE. He went to the country.

NORA. I saw it in your face.

KRISTINE. He'll be back tomorrow night, I left a note.

NORA. You shouldn't have. Maybe it's best to just sit here and wait for the most beautiful thing. In a way it's a joy…

KRISTINE. What beautiful thing?

NORA. Go join them, I'll be there in a minute.

>(**KRISTINE** *exits.)*

>(**NORA** *stands still for a moment, listening to the laughter and voices from the next room. She fixes her hair, preparing herself to go in.)*

>(*She looks at her watch. Calculates under her breath.)*

Seven and twenty-four. Thirty-one hours to live.

>(**TORVALD** *appears.)*

TORVALD. What's keeping my pretty bird?

(**NORA** *turns to him.*)

NORA. Here she is.

End of Act Two

ACT THREE

(**KRISTINE** *is alone onstage. Music can be heard from upstairs.*)

(**KRISTINE** *is waiting anxiously, trying to distract herself.*)

(*Shift.* **KROGSTAD** *stands before her.*)

KRISTINE. Come in, no one's here.

(**KROGSTAD** *stays there uncertainly.*)

KROGSTAD. I got your note.

KRISTINE. Thanks for coming, I need to talk to you.

KROGSTAD. Here?

KRISTINE. It's impossible where I'm staying – come in. No one's here, they're at a party upstairs.

KROGSTAD. Really. They're dancing tonight?

KRISTINE. Why shouldn't they be?

(*A pause. He's waiting to find out why he's been summoned.*)

Can we talk?

KROGSTAD. About what?

KRISTINE. Well there's a lot we should discuss –

KROGSTAD. I can't think of a single thing.

---

*A license to produce *A Doll's House* does not include a performance license for any third-party or copyrighted music or recordings. Licensees should create their own, or use music in the public domain.

KRISTINE. That's because you never really understood when I –

KROGSTAD. Understood what? You dumped me when a better offer came along, not a lot to understand.

KRISTINE. Do you think that was easy for me?

KROGSTAD. Yes, fairly.

KRISTINE. You really believe that?

KROGSTAD. Well yes, because you wrote me a cold little note –

KRISTINE. If I had to end things with you then I thought the kindest thing was to destroy your feelings for me, let you hate me –

KROGSTAD. That's even worse, if you did care about me but you chose money.

KRISTINE. I had a sick mother and two little brothers, you weren't making any money at all back then – sorry, but you weren't, and I didn't know what else to –

KROGSTAD. That doesn't excuse it, you didn't have the right to break your promise to me like that.

KRISTINE. Well, I don't know. I've wondered that, ever since.

(A pause.)

KROGSTAD. When I lost you it was like the ground slid out from under my feet. I could have made something of myself, I was on my way to doing that. Now look at me, I'm shipwrecked.

KRISTINE. Maybe I can help.

KROGSTAD. Help? You stole my job.

KRISTINE. I had no idea until today, I swear, I didn't know it was your job Mr. Helmer offered me.

KROGSTAD. So will you give it up now that you know?

KRISTINE. That wouldn't do you any good.

KROGSTAD. It would be a nice gesture, though.

KRISTINE. I've learned the hard way that it's important to be practical.

KROGSTAD. And I've learned the hard way not to trust what people say. Especially you.

KRISTINE. That's fair. Let me start over.

KROGSTAD. I should get back home –

KRISTINE. Nils, when you said you were "shipwrecked," I recognized that.

KROGSTAD. Yeah well it's pretty obvious.

KRISTINE. No, I mean, I feel the same way. I have no one to care for, no one to care about.

KROGSTAD. You made your own bed.

KRISTINE. Fine, you're right, but what if...what if you and I, two shipwrecked people...

(He looks at her, afraid to be hopeful.)

KROGSTAD. Don't do this to me again.

KRISTINE. Why do you think I came to the city?

KROGSTAD. Not for me. I don't believe you.

KRISTINE. I've been so lonely. My whole life I've worked, I've found meaning in taking care of other people. Now I have no one –

KROGSTAD. That doesn't mean that you want to be with me. This is just pride, some grand, dramatic self-sacrifice –

KRISTINE. Have you ever known me to be dramatic?

I want to be with you. I do.

(He's still terrified to believe what's happening.)

KROGSTAD. Are you, uh. You're aware of my past.

KRISTINE. Completely.

KROGSTAD. You know what people think about me?

KRISTINE. You said a little while ago that with me you could have become someone else.

KROGSTAD. I know I could have.

KRISTINE. So maybe it's not too late.

KROGSTAD. Kristine...I need to tell you –

(The music changes upstairs.)

KRISTINE. It's her dance, you have to go –

KROGSTAD. What?

KRISTINE. When this song is over, they'll come down.

KROGSTAD. I'll go – but I have to tell you what I did to your friend, and I'm sure it'll change how you feel –

KRISTINE. I know everything.

KROGSTAD. You do?

KRISTINE. I know you only did it out of despair.

KROGSTAD. I wish I could take it back.

KRISTINE. You could...your letter is still in the box.

KROGSTAD. Are you sure?

KRISTINE. Very sure. But...

(He looks at her searchingly.)

KROGSTAD. Kristine...if everything you just said to me was...if you're just doing this to save your friend, please tell me. I really need to know.

KRISTINE. I sacrificed what I wanted for other people once, I'm not going to make the same mistake again.

(An emotionally full pause.)

KROGSTAD. When they come downstairs, I'll ask for my letter back.

KRISTINE. No –

KROGSTAD. I'll say I lost my temper about getting fired and now that I've calmed down I'm embarrassed –

KRISTINE. No, I don't want you to do that. In the last twenty-four hours I've seen incredible things in this house. The two of them have to reach a full understanding, the lies have to stop.

KROGSTAD. If you think that's best. But there's one thing I can do right away –

(End of music and applause from upstairs.)

KRISTINE. The dance is over, go!

KROGSTAD. I'll wait for you downstairs.

KRISTINE. Good, you can walk me home.

KROGSTAD. I've never been this happy.

*(**KROGSTAD** exits.)*

*(**KRISTINE** looks after him, happy, full.)*

*(The noise from the party gets louder as **TORVALD** and **NORA** enter, him half carrying her. He's a bit drunk.)*

NORA. No!

TORVALD. Come on...

NORA. Not yet, it's still so early! One more hour.

TORVALD. We had an agreement, remember? Come on, baby. It's freezing out here, in you go.

NORA. Nooooo...

(He leads her, still resisting, into the room, perhaps kisses her.)

KRISTINE. Hello.

NORA. *(Startled.)* Kristine!

TORVALD. You're here late.

KRISTINE. Sorry, I had to see Nora all dressed up.

NORA. You've been sitting here waiting for me?

KRISTINE. I got here after you'd already gone upstairs, so. I really wanted to see you.

TORVALD. Well take a good look. Worth the price of admission, right?

KRISTINE. She's stunning.

TORVALD. That was the general consensus at the party. But she's also stubborn, I regret to say I almost had to drag her out of there by force –

NORA. You're going to regret you didn't let me stay longer.

TORVALD. *(To* **KRISTINE.***)* You see? So she finishes her dance, it was a huge hit – I've seen her do better, but nobody else would have known it was a little looser and wilder than that dance is technically supposed to – but it doesn't matter, everybody loved it, huge response. And should I have let her stay after that? Diminish the effect? No, we left 'em wanting more, acknowledged the applause, thanked the host and – poof! The beautiful apparition vanished. After all these years I still haven't been able to teach Nora how to make a dramatic exit, she always wants to draw it – is it hot in here?

(He goes, perhaps to take off his jacket.)

*(***NORA** *turns to* **KRISTINE.***)*

NORA. So?

KRISTINE. I talked to him. Nora – you have to tell Torvald everything.

NORA. *(Dully.)* I knew it.

KRISTINE. Krogstad isn't going to do anything, but you still have to tell him.

NORA. I can't.

KRISTINE. Then the letter will.

(**NORA** *nods. She takes* **KRISTINE**'s *hand.)*

NORA. Thank you, I know what I have to do.

(**TORVALD** *returns, eager for* **KRISTINE** *to leave.)*

TORVALD. So! Have you taken a good look?

KRISTINE. Yes, I'll go now.

TORVALD. So soon? Is that your knitting?

KRISTINE. Oh thank you, I would have forgotten it.

TORVALD. So you knit?

KRISTINE. Avidly.

TORVALD. Have you ever thought about embroidery, as an alternative?

KRISTINE. Not really, why?

TORVALD. There's something almost balletic about embroidery – you hold it with your left hand and your right hand moves in and out gracefully, like this –

KRISTINE. Huh.

TORVALD. Whereas knitting –

(*He imitates a hunched over knitting posture.)*

You're all elbows. You know? Just an observation. That was excellent champagne they served up there.

KRISTINE. Well, good night, Nora. Don't be stubborn.

TORVALD. Well said!

KRISTINE. Good night, Mr. Helmer.

TORVALD. Good night! Will you be okay getting home? I could – but it's not too far, right?

KRISTINE. I'm fine.

TORVALD. Good night, take care!

(**KRISTINE** *exits.*)

Oh my God she's so boring. I thought she'd never leave.

NORA. Are you exhausted?

TORVALD. Wide awake. You? You look wiped out.

NORA. I'm very tired. I'll sleep soon.

TORVALD. See? I was right to get you out of there.

NORA. Well, you're always right.

TORVALD. Rank was in a good mood tonight.

NORA. Was he? I didn't get to talk to him.

TORVALD. I didn't either, really, but I haven't seen him look so happy in a long time.

(*He moves closer to her.*)

It doesn't get old. Coming home to you, I mean. You're so beautiful.

NORA. Don't look at me like that.

TORVALD. Why not? Why can't I look at my baby? Listen, the guests are leaving. Soon the whole house will be quiet.

NORA. I hope so.

TORVALD. When we're at a party like that – do you know why I stay across the room and don't talk to you? And just look at you once in a while, but I can't let anyone catch me looking? Do you know why I do that? I'm pretending we're secret lovers, and no one can know there's anything between us.

NORA. That's very sweet, that you're always thinking of me.

TORVALD. And when we leave together, I pretend we just got married, and it's going to be our first time. I'm going to slip off your shawl, and touch your shoulders, your neck, your back…it's the first time I'm alone with you, and you're shaking, and I'm shaking…when you were dancing, I couldn't take it, I wanted you so bad, that's why I needed to get you home –

NORA. Stop.

TORVALD. Oh, is that how we're playing –

NORA. I'm not playing, I don't want this.

(He stops, surprised, affronted.)

TORVALD. What? What do you mean?

RANK. *(Offstage.)* It's me!

TORVALD. Damn it.

RANK. *(Offstage.)* Can I stop in for a second?

TORVALD. It's social hour, apparently.

(Calling out.)

Come in!

*(**RANK** enters.)*

Hello! Nice of you to drop by on your way out.

RANK. I thought I heard your voice, hope I'm not interrupting anything.

TORVALD. No!

RANK. Well, here you both are. In this room I love. It's so cozy here with you two.

TORVALD. You seemed pretty cozy upstairs too.

RANK. I was. Good wine, I thought.

TORVALD. Especially the champagne.

RANK. I noticed that too. I put back some champagne.

NORA. So did Torvald.

RANK. Oh yeah?

NORA. That's why he's in such a giddy mood.

RANK. He deserves it, he worked hard today.

TORVALD. No I didn't.

RANK. Well, *I* did.

NORA. Did you conduct a scientific experiment today?

RANK. Exactly.

TORVALD. Have you been teaching my wife about science?

NORA. Was it a...positive result?

RANK. Very positive. The best possible.

NORA. *(A sigh of relief.)* Oh, good!

RANK. For both the doctor and patient. Certainty.

NORA. *(Concerned now, searchingly.)* Certainty?

RANK. Yes. The test was conclusive.

(Knowledge passes between them.)

So I think I deserved to let loose a little tonight, don't you?

NORA. I'm glad you did.

TORVALD. Me too, but you'll pay for it tomorrow morning.

RANK. Well, you don't get something for nothing in this life.

NORA. *(To* **RANK**.*)* You've always loved costume parties, haven't you?

RANK. As long as there are plenty of creative costumes.

NORA. Listen, what should we go as next time?

TORVALD. She's already on to the next one.

RANK. You and me? That's easy. You'll be Fortune's Child.

TORVALD. Try coming up with a costume for that.

RANK. She'll go just as she is, as herself.

TORVALD. Aw, very nicely said. Any idea what you'll be?

RANK. I know exactly, old friend. I'll be invisible.

TORVALD. Also hard to pull off.

RANK. You must have heard of the hat of invisibility. It's a big, black hat – you put it on and then no one can see you anymore.

> (**TORVALD** *laughs slightly, not knowing what to make of this conversation.)*

TORVALD. Okay then...

RANK. I forgot why I came. Can I have a cigar, one of the good ones?

TORVALD. My pleasure.

NORA. Let me light it.

RANK. Thank you.

And...goodbye!

TORVALD. Good night, buddy.

NORA. Sleep well, Peter.

RANK. Thank you for that wish.

NORA. Say it back to me.

>   (*He stops.*)

RANK. All right. Sleep well, Nora. Thank you for the light.

>   (*Looking at each of them again, he leaves.*)

>   (*A pause.*)

TORVALD. He's sloshed.

NORA. I guess.

>   (**TORVALD** *goes.*)

What are you doing?

TORVALD. The mailbox is full, if I don't empty it there won't be room for the paper tomorrow.

NORA. You want to work tonight?

TORVALD. No, but I – what is –?

NORA. What's wrong?

TORVALD. Something's wrong with the lock.

NORA. Really?

TORVALD. It's like something's stuck in the – it's one of your hair pins.

NORA. It must have been the kids.

TORVALD. Well tell them to keep their hands off the mailbox.

It doesn't matter, I got it.

>   (*He reenters.*)

You see how it's piled up?

>   (*She watches him.*)

NORA. Torvald, before you –

TORVALD. That's weird, Rank left two business cards. He must have dropped them on his way out.

NORA. Did he write anything on them?

TORVALD. There's a black X over his name. Look. That's creepy. It's like he's announcing his own death or something.

NORA. He is.

TORVALD. Did he say something to you?

NORA. He's dying, he's going to shut himself away now. No visitors.

TORVALD. Oh, no. I knew I couldn't keep him forever, but I didn't think it would be this soon. And he's just hiding away, like a wounded animal?

NORA. If it has to happen, maybe it's best to do it without words. Don't you think?

TORVALD. He was such a part of our home, I can barely imagine what it'll be like without him. That cynical, depressive bastard – he was like the cloudy backdrop to our sunny lives. Well, he's been suffering for a long time, maybe it's for the best.

For us, too. It's just you and me now.

(He holds her.)

Oh baby. I can't hold you tight enough.

Did you know that sometimes I fantasize that you're in danger, real danger, so that I get to risk my life to save you?

NORA. You should read your letters now.

TORVALD. That can wait, tonight I want to be with you –

NORA. Right after hearing your friend is dying?

(He stops.)

TORVALD. No, you're right. You're right. We're both upset, having morbid thoughts. We should sleep in separate rooms tonight.

NORA. Good night, Torvald.

TORVALD. Good night, little bird. Sleep well.

> *(He kisses her.)*

I'll go read my letters.

> *(He exits.)*

> *(She looks after him, waiting a moment to move.)*

NORA. Goodbye. Goodbye, Ivar, Emmy.

> *(She begins to move, stops.)*

Freezing water, all black…It'll be over soon.

> *(She looks again toward* **TORVALD**.*)*

Now he knows. Goodbye!

TORVALD. *(Offstage.)* Nora!

> *(**TORVALD** reenters.)*

Do you know what this says?

NORA. Yes – let me out.

TORVALD. Where are you going?

NORA. Don't try to save me!

TORVALD. It's true? What he wrote in here? Answer me! This cannot possibly be true!

NORA. It's true. I've loved you more than anything in the world.

TORVALD. I don't want to hear your excuses.

NORA. Torvald –

TORVALD. What have you done?

NORA. I won't let you take the blame for / this!

TORVALD. *(He speaks with cold fury.)* You stupid bitch. Explain yourself to me. Do you understand what you've done? Hm? Do you have any understanding at all?

(She stares at him.)

NORA. Yes. I think I'm finally starting to understand.

TORVALD. How can this be happening to me? I loved you. I cherished you. All this time, I've been living with a liar. A *criminal*. I feel sick.

*(**NORA** keeps staring at him.)*

And I should've known it. You're your father's daughter. Don't interrupt me. You're just like him, no religion, no moral compass, no sense of duty. I overlooked his faults for your sake – and this is what I get.

NORA. Yes, this is what you get.

TORVALD. I'm never going to be happy again. You've destroyed my future. Oh my God, I'm at the mercy of that loser, he's my boss now, he can do whatever he wants to me and I better not complain. Because of *you*. Because of your reckless, stupid –

NORA. Once I'm gone from this world he won't be able to –

TORVALD. No grand gestures, please, Nora, you learned that from your daddy too – you're all talk. How would it help me at all if you were "gone from this world," huh? You think that would stop him from telling everyone what you did? Then I'd be suspected of encouraging you, maybe even pushing you over the ledge myself. When the truth is I have carried you on my back for eight years. Do you realize what you've done to me?

NORA. *(Clear and calm.)* Yes.

TORVALD. This is unreal. But we need a plan. Sit down. Sit. Down. I have to give him what he wants. I can't let this information get out, no matter what it costs. And in terms of you and me, nothing has changed – I mean that's what it has to look like. But only to the outside world. You'll still live here but I can't trust you with the children, obviously, you have to stay away from them. I can't believe I'm standing here saying this to you when I've loved you so much –

(Catching himself.)

But that's over now. Happiness isn't a luxury we can afford anymore, all we can do is preserve appearances.

(The doorbell rings.)

Oh my God. He's here. At this hour –? Hide, Nora. Say you're sick.

(But she doesn't move. Shift – a minute later.)

He left a letter. You can't have it, I'll read it myself.

NORA. Go ahead.

TORVALD. *(Pausing before opening it.)* This could be the end for us.

(He steels himself before reading. Then –)

(A cry of joy.)

Nora!

(She looks at him.)

Wait, let me read it again to make sure...yes, it's real, I'm saved! Nora, I'm saved.

NORA. What about me?

TORVALD. You too, of course. He returned your contract. He apologized – said he, uh – "regrets and repents that he let a tragedy in his own life" – anyway doesn't matter, we're saved, we're free!

In a few days this will all seem like a bad dream. There. It doesn't exist, maybe it never did. He wrote that since Christmas Eve you – oh, Nora. You've had a horrible three days.

NORA. I've been fighting a hard battle.

TORVALD. And you were actually thinking of...

We're never going to talk about it again. It's over, baby. It's over. Hey, are you okay? I think you're in shock. Listen to me. I forgive you. I know you did what you did because you love me.

NORA. That's true.

TORVALD. You just didn't understand what made it so wrong, and that's not your fault, you don't know how to make judgments like that. That's okay, because I'm here. Trust that I'm strong enough to hold you up and guide you, because I am. I'm sorry about what I said before, I was just – I felt like the world was closing in on me, and I...but Nora, I completely forgive you. I swear.

NORA. Thank you.

(She stands and exits.)

TORVALD. Where are you going?

NORA. *(Offstage.)* To take off my costume.

(A brief pause.)

TORVALD. Good idea! Get comfortable, take a breath.

(Pause.)

TORVALD. I love our house. That was awful, for a second there, to look around this place we made together and think it was all just...but it's giving me that homey feeling again, there's a feeling I get every time I walk in the door, knowing I'm home, all of this is mine, and you're here, our children...

> *(Pause.)*

It's true what they say, forgiveness feels good. I think I even love you a little more than I did half an hour ago. Because there's this new tenderness, too, that's almost like...it's almost like I feel with Ivar, or Emmy when they've done something wrong and they cry and cry...

> *(Pause.)*

I'm here, Nora. I'm here for you, and you never have to be afraid again.

> *(**NORA** reenters.)*

You're not going to bed? You changed?

NORA. Yes, I changed.

TORVALD. Why, it's so late –

NORA. I'm not sleeping tonight.

TORVALD. But –

NORA. And it's not that late. Sit down. We have a lot to talk about.

TORVALD. What's going on?

NORA. Sit down, this will take a while.

TORVALD. You're scaring me a little. I'm not sure I understand –

NORA. Exactly, you don't understand me. And I've never understood you, until tonight.

TORVALD. What does that mean?

NORA. Do you notice something right now, about the way we're sitting here?

TORVALD. What would I notice?

NORA. We've been married for eight years. Do you think it's striking that this is the first time we're having a real conversation?

TORVALD. "Real," in what sense?

NORA. In eight years we've never really talked about serious things.

TORVALD. Should I have shared every worry with you, even when you couldn't do anything about it?

NORA. I'm not talking about that. I'm saying we've never sat down together and tried to get to the bottom of something.

TORVALD. ...and you would have liked that?

NORA. This is my point. You've never understood me. I've been very, very wronged. By Papa, and then by you.

TORVALD. You mean by the two people who loved you most?

NORA. You never loved me. You just enjoyed being in love with me.

TORVALD. How can you say that?

NORA. Because it's the truth. Back home, Papa told me all his opinions about things and so I had the same opinions, or if I didn't I kept them to myself. He called me his little doll and he played with me just like I played with my dolls. Then I came to your house –

TORVALD. You mean, we got married.

NORA. *(Undisturbed.)* I mean I went from Papa's house to yours, and I learned about your tastes and then I acquired the same tastes myself – or I pretended to – I honestly don't know anymore, maybe it was both. When I look back, I realize how poor I've been, living from hand to mouth, performing tricks for you, Torvald. You and Papa have wronged me terribly. That's why I haven't made anything of my life.

TORVALD. That's unfair. Haven't you been happy here?

NORA. No. I thought I was, but I wasn't.

TORVALD. Not happy?

NORA. No, just cheerful. You've been very sweet to me. But I was just your doll wife, like I was Papa's doll child. Our children became my dolls. I thought it was fun when you played with me just like they thought it was fun when I played with them. That was our marriage, Torvald.

TORVALD. Listen...there may be a kernel of truth in what you're saying, even if it's wildly exaggerated. But you're right, things need to change around here. Playtime is over, it's time for education.

NORA. Whose education? Mine or the kids'?

TORVALD. Both.

NORA. *(Somewhat sorry for him.)* Oh, Torvald. You're in no position to teach me anything.

TORVALD. How can you say that?

NORA. And I'm not qualified to educate the children.

TORVALD. Nora, that's –

NORA. Didn't you just say that a few minutes ago? That you can't trust me with our children?

TORVALD. I was angry, can we please move past that?

NORA. No, you meant what you said. I'm not prepared for that work, there's something I have to do first. Educate myself. And you can't help me with that, I have to do it alone. And that's why I'm leaving you.

TORVALD. What?

NORA. I have to figure out who I am and what I'm doing in this world. I can't live with you anymore.

TORVALD. Nora!

NORA. Kristine will let me stay with her tonight.

TORVALD. You've lost your mind. I won't let you.

NORA. I won't take anything of yours, just what I own.

TORVALD. This is complete insanity.

NORA. I'll go home to where I grew up, it'll be easier for me to find work there.

TORVALD. You are so naïve –

NORA. That's why I need to get some experience.

TORVALD. You're going to leave your home, your husband, your *children*? Do you know what people will say?

NORA. I can't worry about that. I just know this is what I need to do.

TORVALD. And it's that simple, huh? To just walk away from your most sacred duties –?

NORA. To you and the children, you mean?

TORVALD. Yes, I do mean that, but maybe you no longer consider those sacred?

NORA. I have another equally sacred responsibility.

TORVALD. To –

NORA. Myself.

(Pause.)

TORVALD. Nora. You are a mother. You are a wife. You / can't just –

NORA. I'm a human being. Just like you are. Or at least I'm trying to become one. I know you're right, Torvald, according to most people and what it says in the books. But I can't rely on that anymore, I have to think things through for myself.

TORVALD. You can't rely on me anymore, okay. What about your religion? Are you throwing that away too?

NORA. My religion? Oh Torvald, I have no idea what religion even is.

TORVALD. Okay. Okay. What about your conscience? Do you still have one of those? Any moral feelings whatsoever? Or no?

NORA. *(Thoughtfully.)* That's a good question. I don't exactly know, I'm very confused about morality. I only know that I don't agree with your views about it. I've recently learned that the law is different from what I thought – that a woman doesn't have the right to protect her dying father or to save her husband's life. Could the law be right about that? I don't believe it.

TORVALD. That's just a childish...you don't understand the society you live in.

NORA. No, I don't. So now I have to go find out if society is right or if I am.

TORVALD. I'm wondering if you have a fever, or this is some kind of psychotic episode –

NORA. I've never felt as clear and sure as I do right now.

TORVALD. And when you're clear and sure, you leave your husband and children.

NORA. Right.

TORVALD. There's only one explanation for this.

NORA. What?

TORVALD. You don't love me anymore.

NORA. No. That's true.

TORVALD. *(Deeply hurt.)* Nora...

NORA. It's very painful to say that to you, because you've been so kind to me. But I can't help it. I don't love you anymore. That's why I can't keep living here.

TORVALD. Can you explain to me how I lost your love?

NORA. Yes. It was tonight when the most beautiful thing didn't happen. Then I realized you're not who I thought you were.

TORVALD. I don't understand what you're saying.

NORA. I waited for eight years. I know beautiful things don't happen every day, and I was happy to wait. But then this crushing wave came at me, and – I was so sure that it would finally happen. When Krogstad's letter was out there – it never occurred to me that you would let that man walk all over us, I was sure, I was positive you would say, "go ahead, tell everyone." And then –

TORVALD. Yeah, what then? After I'd exposed you to public humiliation –

NORA. Well, then I thought, and again I was positive, that you would stand up and take the blame. And say you were the guilty one.

TORVALD. But Nora –

NORA. Of course I would never let you do that, I'd never accept that sacrifice from you. But who would believe me over you? That was the most beautiful thing that terrified me, that I was hoping for. And to prevent it I was ready to take my own life.

TORVALD. I would have worked like a dog for you, Nora. I would have accepted any hardship, any sorrow, but – I'm sorry. No man sacrifices his dignity for the person he loves.

NORA. Hundreds of thousands of women have done that.

TORVALD. You sound like a child.

NORA. Maybe. But you sound like someone I can't share my life with. When that scare was over – *your* scare, I mean, what was threatening *you* – then suddenly it was like nothing had happened. I was your little bird again, your doll, except I was even more helpless than before and you liked that even better. Torvald, in that moment, I realized that for eight years I've been living here with a stranger, and I had two children...with a... it's unbearable, I could tear myself to pieces.

(Long pause.)

TORVALD. I see. Oh, Nora, you suddenly seem so far away. But don't you think we can reach each other –?

NORA. Not now.

TORVALD. I have the strength to change.

NORA. Maybe, if your doll is taken away from you.

TORVALD. But I can't imagine being without you. I can't even comprehend...

NORA. That's why it has to happen.

(She gets ready to go.)

TORVALD. Not now. Nora please, wait until the morning.

NORA. I can't spend the night in a stranger's house.

TORVALD. But – couldn't we try living here together like brother and sister?

NORA. That wouldn't last long and you know it.

Goodbye, Torvald. I don't want to see the children. I know they're in good hands. Better than mine, right now, anyway.

TORVALD. But maybe someday –?

NORA. I have no idea, who knows what my life will look like.

TORVALD. But you'll still be my wife. Wherever you are, whoever you become –

NORA. Listen – I'm leaving your house and that releases you from all obligations toward me. Isn't that the law? Either way, I release you, you shouldn't feel bound to me in any way, we both have to have total freedom. Here's your ring. Give me mine.

TORVALD. Do we really have to...?

> *(She waits.)*

NORA. There, it's done.

Anne-Marie knows how to run the house – better than I do.

TORVALD. Nora.

> *(He moves toward her to embrace or kiss her – she takes a step away.)*

Will you ever think of me?

> *(Pause. She collects herself.)*

NORA. Often. You and the children and our home here. Yes.

TORVALD. Can I write to you?

NORA. No.

TORVALD. Let me send you / some money.

NORA. No.

TORVALD. But if you need help –

NORA. I can't accept help from strangers.

TORVALD. Nora. One day, isn't it possible...I won't be a stranger to you anymore?

NORA. Oh, Torvald. That would take the most beautiful thing of all.

TORVALD. What beautiful thing? Tell me.

NORA. We would both have to change so much that – I'm sorry, I don't believe in beautiful things happening anymore.

TORVALD. I want to believe, though. Say it. Change so much that –

NORA. That our relationship could become a marriage. Goodbye.

(She exits.)

TORVALD. Nora...

(He waits, thinking she might turn around. He weeps. Then, suddenly, hope begins to fill him.)

The most beautiful thing –?

(The door slams.)

End of Play

OPTIONAL TARANTELLA SCENE

NORA. Wait! I can't perform tomorrow if I don't rehearse with you.

TORVALD. Are you really that nervous?

NORA. Unbearably. There's time to rehearse before dinner, come on. Direct me, like you always do.

TORVALD. Okay, at your service.

> (**TORVALD** *begins to play the piano or a recording.**)

> (**RANK** *claps along as* **NORA** *starts to dance.*)

Slow down, you're ahead.

NORA. I can't help it.

TORVALD. A little less violently.

NORA. I can't. It has to be like this.

> (**TORVALD** *stops playing the music.*)

TORVALD. Stop!

> (*She does.*)

Listen.

> (**TORVALD** *starts playing the music again.* **RANK** *claps. She starts to dance.*)

Not yet, just listen first, feel the rhythm.

> (*She closes her eyes, trying to follow his instructions, but breaks out dancing.*)

Wait, slow down...

---

* A license to produce *A Doll's House* does not include a performance license for any third-party or copyrighted music or recordings. Licensees should create their own, or use music in the public domain.

(**NORA** *dances more and more wildly.*)

TORVALD. Easy, easy. Easy!

(**KRISTINE** *enters, stares.*)

KRISTINE. Oh –

NORA. Kristine! Look at me!

(**TORVALD** *stops the music again but* **NORA** *is still dancing and* **RANK** *keeps clapping.*)

TORVALD. Nora, this is not life or death!

NORA. *(Biting his head off.)* Yes it is!

TORVALD. *(To* **RANK** *who is still clapping.)* Stop.

(*Even with no beat,* **NORA** *keeps dancing, ever wilder. Like an external force is thrashing her body around.*)

Stop, stop, stop, stop, stop!

(*He puts his arms around her, subduing her. She finally stops.*)

(*She catches her breath.*)

Well. You certainly need a lot of rehearsal.